ME,
MYSELF,
AND
I

ME, MYSELF, AND I

BY GLADYS YESSAYAN CRETAN

Illustrated by
DON BOLOGNESE

William Morrow and Company   New York

ME,
MYSELF,
AND
I

When I look in the mirror,
who do I see?
Not just me.
No.
I see different things.

Bravest of all.
A trainer of lions.
An astronaut.
Or sometimes I see a clown.
A happy-sad clown.
Once I was a giant. Immense. Scowling.

AND ONCE I WAS A KNIGHT IN ARMOR

I think I must look different
to the milkman.
He calls me Tiger.
Another thing....
When I shoot an arrow
into the air,
I shout, "I'm Robin Hood."
And I am. I am.
But right then

my mother calls,
and there goes Robin Hood,
the hero of Sherwood Forest,
defender of the poor.
There he goes, with a note in his hand…
to the butcher.
And the butcher doesn't see Robin Hood.
Who does he see?
Does he see me?
He says, "Hi, Sport!"

Coming home, my friends want to try a new baseball bat.
(I put the meat down for only a minute.)

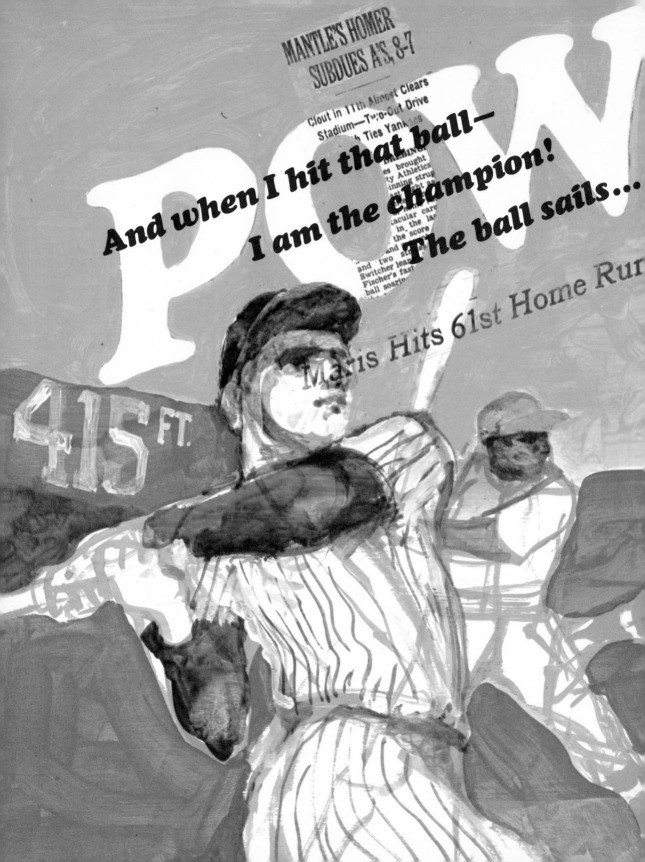

And when I hit that ball—
I am the champion!
The ball sails...

Out...Out...Out
over the heads of thousands of people.
Over the stands.
I run around the bases,
run, run to the roar
of the voices
and the clapping of the hands.
I am the best ballplayer
they ever saw.
I take the meat home
to my mother, and I say,
"Call me Champ."

396

Sometimes I am a cowboy.
For hours. For days.
I am the fastest gun in the West.
I'm strong.

Other times
I am the bad guy.
I'm tough.
I am two different cowboys.

Some days I am a captain.
 Captain of the guard.
  Captain of the ship.
   Captain of the Army.
    I'm in charge. I know things.

      But....
      Some days I sit still. Stone-still.
      And I wonder. I puzzle over things.
      Where does the captain go?
      The one who knows.
      Besides the people and names,
      I can be other things.
      For instance.
      Once I was lying on the grass,
      looking up.

I saw a plane. Silver blue.
Climbing. Climbing.
I held my breath.

I wasn't the pilot. Not exactly.
And I wasn't the plane. Not quite.
But I was there.
And all the time the grass was tickling my elbows.
Then one day I saw a horse racing,
and I felt I was that horse.
No. I <u>knew</u> I was that horse.
I wasn't the jockey.
I wasn't the trainer.
And not anyone watching.
I was that one special brown-black horse.
And it was hot!
I liked running against the wind.

When I dive deep into the water, I am a different me.
I glide. I slide. Quickly.
In the deep world I am a mystery.
Then I float up, up, and I see my friends again.
We splash and we laugh.
They don't see the mysterious me.
When I am out of the water.

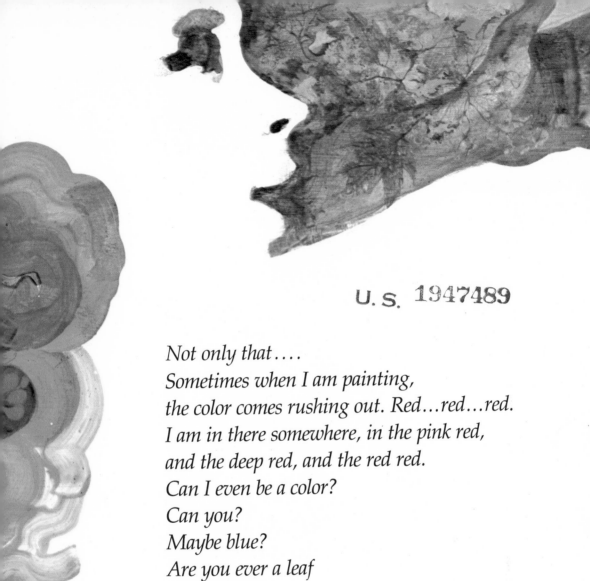

U. S. 1947489

Not only that . . . .
Sometimes when I am painting,
the color comes rushing out. Red . . . red . . . red.
I am in there somewhere, in the pink red,
and the deep red, and the red red.
Can I even be a color?
Can you?
Maybe blue?
Are you ever a leaf
when it falls?
I watch. I feel it settle. I feel right.

Even music.
  Especially a march
    that rushes and swirls and twirls around me.
      I am in it. I am in the sound.
        I move on it. Move in it.
          When the music is over, there is a quiet.
            A coming back.
              I look down and see my brown shoes.
                I tie that shoelace again.
                  When I look in the mirror,
                    who do I see?

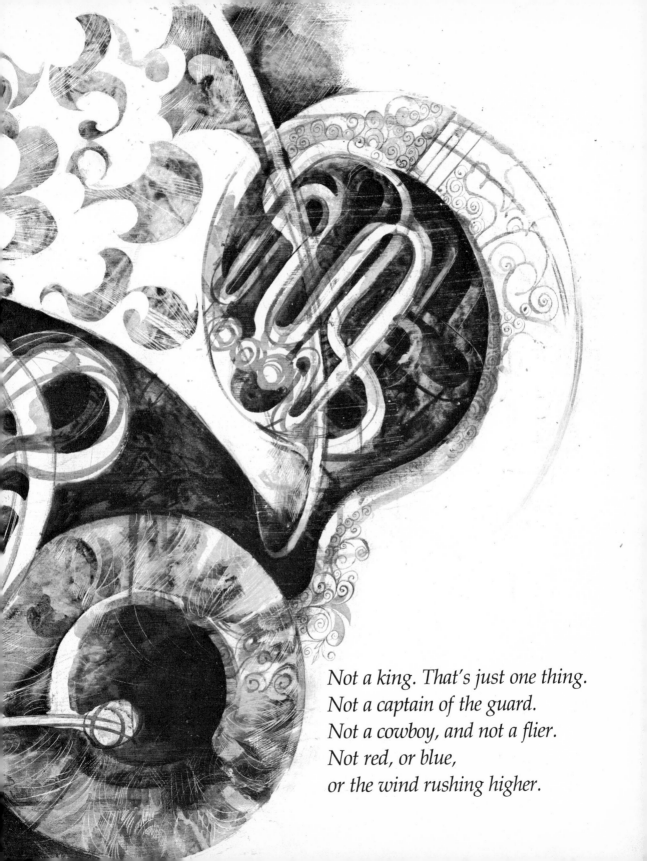

Not a king. That's just one thing.
Not a captain of the guard.
Not a cowboy, and not a flier.
Not red, or blue,
or the wind rushing higher.

I see all these things.
I am whatever I want to be.
But especially,
particularly,
positively….

About the author

Born in Reedley, California, Gladys Yessayan Cretan went to elementary and secondary school there, and then attended the University of California in Berkeley. She has traveled extensively in her home state, and now she and her husband live in San Mateo. Their two sons are attending college. She is interested in music, in community activities, especially those involving teen-agers, and she recently has had several picture books published.

About the artist

Don Bolognese, a noted children's book illustrator, found a personal inspiration in Mrs. Cretan's text that has expressed itself in his imaginative artwork. "When I read this manuscript," he says, "I was struck by its similarity to remembrances of my own childhood. Like most young boys, I had a vivid and active fantasy life, and that boy is still lurking somewhere inside of me. Especially so on spring-green days, or on a dreamy summer day when every park becomes Camelot and each breeze a call to adventure." Mr. Bolognese, a resident of Brooklyn, N. Y., is married and has two children.